Editor - Zachary Rau
Contributing Editors - Steven Starkweather and Ian Mayer
Graphic Designer and Letterer - Peter Sattler
Cover Designer - Louis Csontos
Graphic Artist - Tomás Montalvo-Lagos and John Lo

Digital Imaging Manager - Chris Buford
Production Managers - Jennifer Miller and Mutsumi Miyazaki
Senior Designer - Anna Kernbaum
Senior Editor - Elizabeth Hurchalla
Managing Editor - Lindsey Johnston
VP of Production - Ron Klamert
Publisher & Editor in Chief - Mike Kiley
President & C.O.O. - John Parker
C.E.O. - Stuart Levy

E-mail: info@TOKYOPOP.com
Come visit us online at www.TOKYOPOP.com

A 🅒 **TOKYOPOP** Cine-Manga® Book
TOKYOPOP Inc.
5900 Wilshire Blvd., Suite 2000
Los Angeles, CA 90036

SpongeBob Squarepants: Who's Hungry?

ISBN: 1-59532-889-0

First TOKYOPOP® printing: May 2006

10 9 8 7 6 5 4 3 2 1

Printed in the USA

NICK

SpongeBob SquarePants

SPONGEBOB SQUAREPANTS: An optimistic and friendly sea sponge who lives in a pineapple with his snail, Gary, and works as a fry cook at The Krusty Krab. He loves his job and is always looking on the bright side of everything.

PATRICK STAR: A starfish who is SpongeBob's best friend and neighbor.

GARY: Spongebob's pet snail. Meows like a cat.

PLANKTON: The owner of the Chum Bucket. Plankton's always plotting to steal Mr. Krab's Secret Krabby Patty recipe.

SQUIDWARD TENTACLES: A six-tentacled octopus who works as the cashier at The Krusty Krab. Unlike SpongeBob, Squidward tends to be negative about everything.

MR. KRABS: A crab who owns and runs The Krusty Krab. Mr. Krabs loves money and will do anything to avoid losing it.

SpongeBob SquarePants

WHO'S HUNGRY?

TA-DA!

GREAT BARRIER REEF! THAT PATTY'S SPOILED!

HA HA! MR. KRABS, IT'S NOT TAINTED MEAT! IT'S PAINTED MEAT!

SCOOOORCH!!!

SOB SOB SOB

SNIFF!

WE INTERRUPT THIS PROGRAM FOR AN IMPORTANT NEWS ANNOUNCEMENT. THIS WILD THRONG BEHIND ME IS SCREAMING FOR BIKINI BOTTOM'S NEWEST CULINARY SENSATION. LET'S TAKE A LISTEN.

PRETTY PATTIES?!

THEY MATCH OUR PURSES!

THEY REMIND ME OF HOME!

PRETTY PATTIES RUUUUULE!

41

YOU'RE RIGHT, MR. KRABS. I'M GONNA MAKE SPONGEBOB'S FINAL HOURS THE BEST HE'S EVER HAD!

AND THIS TIME THERE'S GONNA BE LOVE! SO MUCH HE'S GONNA DROWN IN IT!

NOTE TO SELF... WATCH OUT FOR SQUIDWARD.

UH, SPONGEBOB? I FORGOT TO TELL YOU THERE'S A PART TWO TO YOUR GIFT!

PART-TWO, PART-TWO, PART-TWO, PART-TWO, PART-TWO!

UH, PLEASE DON'T DO THAT

BOING! BOING! BOING!

...END OF THE TWILIGHT

...IC LAYER
...Y BIRTH
...AIN POWERED
BRIGADOON
B'TX
CANDIDATE FOR GODDESS, THE
CARDCAPTOR SAKURA
CARDCAPTOR SAKURA - MASTER OF THE CLOW
CHRONICLES OF THE CURSED SWORD
CLAMP SCHOOL DETECTIVES
CLOVER
COMIC PARTY
CORRECTOR YUI
COWBOY BEBOP
COWBOY BEBOP: SHOOTING STAR
CRESCENT MOON
CROSS
CULDCEPT
CYBORG 009
D•N•ANGEL
DEARS
DEMON DIARY
DEMON ORORON, THE
DIGIMON
DIGIMON TAMERS
DIGIMON ZERO TWO
DRAGON HUNTER
DRAGON KNIGHTS
DRAGON VOICE
DREAM SAGA
DUKLYON: CLAMP SCHOOL DEFENDERS
ET CETERA
ETERNITY
FAERIES' LANDING
FLCL
FLOWER OF THE DEEP SLEEP
FORBIDDEN DANCE
FRUITS BASKET
G GUNDAM
GATEKEEPERS
GIRL GOT GAME
GUNDAM SEED ASTRAY
GUNDAM SEED ASTRAY R
GUNDAM WING
GUNDAM WING: BATTLEFIELD OF PACIFISTS
GUNDAM WING: ENDLESS WALTZ
GUNDAM WING: THE LAST OUTPOST (G-UNIT)
HANDS OFF!

HARLEM BEAT
HYPER RUNE
I.N.V.U.
INITIAL D
INSTANT TEEN: JUST ADD NUTS
JING: KING OF BANDITS
JING: KING OF BANDITS - TWILIGHT TALES
JULINE
KARE KANO
KILL ME, KISS ME
KINDAICHI CASE FILES, THE
KING OF HELL
KODOCHA: SANA'S STAGE
LAGOON ENGINE
LEGEND OF CHUN HYANG, THE
LILING-PO
LOVE OR MONEY
MAGIC KNIGHT RAYEARTH I
MAGIC KNIGHT RAYEARTH II
MAN OF MANY FACES
MARMALADE BOY
MARS
MARS: HORSE WITH NO NAME
MINK
MIRACLE GIRLS
MODEL
MOURYOU KIDEN: LEGEND OF THE NYMPH
NECK AND NECK
ONE
ONE I LOVE, THE
PEACH FUZZ
PEACH GIRL
PEACH GIRL: CHANGE OF HEART
PHD: PHANTASY DEGREE
PITA-TEN
PLANET BLOOD
PLANET LADDER
PLANETES
PRESIDENT DAD
PRINCESS AI
PSYCHIC ACADEMY
QUEEN'S KNIGHT, THE
RAGNAROK
RAVE MASTER
REALITY CHECK
REBIRTH
REBOUND
RISING STARS OF MANGA™,THE
SAILOR MOON
SAINT TAIL
SAMURAI GIRL ™ REAL BOUT HIGH SCHOOL

10.19.04Y

ALSO AVAILABLE FROM 😊 TOKYOPOP®

You want it? We got it!
A full range of TOKYOPOP
products are available now at:
www.TOKYOPOP.com/shop

10.19.04Y